HUNGRY NO MORE

Tana Reiff

A Pacemaker® **HOPES** *And* **DREAMS** Book

G.
Pe

Hungry No More

Tana Reiff
AR B.L.: 2.4
Points: 0.5   UG

HOPES *And* DREAMS

Cover photo: Library of Congress
Illustration: Tennessee Dixon

ISBN 0-8224-3680-9
Printed in the United States of America

8 9 10 11 12   07 06 05 04 03

Globe
Fearon

Pearson Learning Group

1-800-321-3106
www.pearsonlearning.com

CONTENTS

CHAPTER 1
Ireland, 1845

The story ended.
Everyone laughed.

"Those were
the good old days,"
said Father Kerry.
"I was young then
and you were
but children."

"You are still
young at heart,"
said Johnny McGee.

"Now tell us more,"
said Mary McGee.
"I like you

to tell stories
when you visit."
She was holding
her little son Terry
on her lap.

"Yes, yes,"
said the old priest.
"Those were
the good days—
in beautiful,
green Ireland.
Each family
kept chickens
and a pig.
They sold eggs.
They made
the pig fat.
Then they sold it, too.
They used the money
to buy
clothes and shoes."

"But now
there is only

the potato,"
said Johnny.

"Only the potato,"
said Father Kerry.
"However,
the potato
is good.
You throw
a few potatoes
on the hot fire,
and that is
your dinner!"

Johnny knew
all about potatoes.
He and Mary
paid rent
to farm potatoes.
They grew
lots of them.
The potatoes grew
no matter what.
They ate potatoes
every day.

Even the roof
of their house
was made of potato plants.
The potato
was their life.
The potato
was everything
to Ireland.

"Thank God
for potatoes,"
said Mary.
"What would we do
without potatoes?"

"Amen,"
said Father Kerry.
"And did you hear
about old Mrs. Cleary?"

"Tell us,"
said Mary McGee.
"You know
what *everyone* is doing!"

Thinking It Over

1. Do you think
   it is smart
   to grow only potatoes?

2. Who do you know
   who always has a story
   to tell?

3. What have you heard
   about "the good old days"?

CHAPTER **2**

The potatoes
had begun
to pop out of the ground.
It looked like
another good year.

But one day
Johnny saw trouble.
Some potato plants
were turning black.
The next day
more plants
were black.

Johnny talked
to some other farmers.
They, too,
were seeing black plants.

Father Kerry
came to visit

that night.
"Everyone around here
has black plants,"
he told Johnny.
"It is a potato rot.
It is killing
all the potato plants.
People are afraid.
Paddy Morgan
even lost the potatoes
he had in store."

"We can get by,"
said Mary.
"We have enough
good potatoes
from last year.
We can get by
one bad year."

And a bad year
it was.
The McGees lost
all their potato plants.

The potatoes
from last year
were not enough
to get by on.
Johnny and Mary
became hungry.
They ate weeds
to stay alive.
They began
to feel weak.
Little Terry
cried all the time.

"Next year
will be better,"
Mary kept saying.

Johnny was glad
when planting time came.
There was hope
in the spring fields.
He watched
as the new shoots
came up.
"It is good

to see green again,"
he said to Mary.

Johnny checked
the potatoes
every day.
One day
the potato plants
were green.
The next day
they were black.

Now there were
no old potatoes
to fall back on.
The whole country
was in trouble.

England sent wheat
to Ireland.
"It is nice
to have this wheat,"
said Mary McGee.
But we only got
a few pounds!

It will not last
very long."

Everyone
was hungry.
Many people died.
Some people left
for England,
Canada, and America.
Some people died
by the side of the road.
Old Mrs. Cleary
stayed in her cottage.
She could do nothing
but wait to die.

"We are hungry,"
Mary told Father Kerry.
"We are worried
about our son.
We might die
just like the others.
Then what would become
of our little Terry?
What shall we do?"

"Hold on,
my children.
Don't leave Ireland,"
begged the priest.
"Things will get better.
We must keep praying
that the potatoes
will come back."

Thinking It Over

1. What would you do
   if you had nothing to eat?

2. Have you ever had to
   "get by" on little or nothing?

3. Why would someone
   "wait to die"?

4. Why do you think
   the priest wants
   Johnny and Mary
   to stay in Ireland?

CHAPTER 3

"I'm sorry,"
said Johnny
to Father Kerry.
"Things are
too far gone.
We will die
if we stay
in Ireland.
We have to
think about
our little boy.
We cannot wait
another year.
There is nothing left
for us to eat.
We are young.
Poor Ireland
is done.
We must get away.
We will go
to America."

"Yes, perhaps
you must go,"
said Father Kerry.
"But it costs less
to go to Canada.
Some people walk
from Canada to
America."

"That is
a very long walk,"
said Johnny.
"We are not
very strong.
It would be better
to go to America.
The American cotton ships
are better
to ride in, too.
The ship
will take us
right to Boston."

So Johnny and Mary
did not pay the rent.
They kept the money

to pay for their trip.
They also took the money
they had once put
inside the roof.
Now money could not buy food.
But it could buy escape.

Father Kerry
saw them off.
"You have
my blessing,"
he said.
"God be with you."

Johnny and Mary
and little Terry
went to Liverpool, England.
There, they boarded
an American cotton ship.
In 40 long days
Johnny and Mary McGee
were in America.

Thinking It Over

1. Which would you have done:
   . . . stayed in Ireland?
   . . . paid less to go to Canada?
   . . . paid more to go to America?

2. Was it right
   for Johnny and Mary
   to use their rent money
   to pay for their trip?

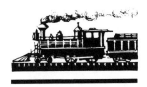

CHAPTER 4

Johnny and Mary
stepped off the boat.

"Welcome to Boston!"
called a man.

"Thank you!"
said Johnny.
"You sound as if
you come from Ireland, too."

"That's right,"
said the man.
"I'm here
to help you greenhorns.
Do you need
a place to live?
I can find it
for you.
Do you need jobs?

I know
where the jobs are.
How can I help?"

    "We only need
a room,"
said Johnny.
"We don't know
if we will stay
in Boston."

    "You'll stay
in the city!"
laughed the man.
"Why go
out to the country?
The land
was no friend to you
in Ireland,
now was it?"

    "No, no, it wasn't,"
said Mary.

    "I'll put you
in a good room

in town,"
said the man.
"And you, Mr.—"

"McGee,"
said Johnny.
"Johnny McGee.
And this is
my wife, Mary."

"My name
is Michael McNair,"
said the man.
He looked at Mary.
She was carrying Terry
in her arms.
"Now isn't that
a fine looking lad
you've got there."

Mary smiled
for the first time.

The man
kept talking.
"Now, Johnny,

you can work
on the railroad.
The work is hard.
But the pay is good.
Fair is fair,
I always say.
And you, Mary,
you can work
in the wool mill.
There's a job
for everyone
here in America!
You'll be well off
before you know it!"

Thinking It Over

1. Do you think
   Johnny and Mary
   should trust
   Michael McNair?

2. What is
   a "greenhorn"?

3. Why do you think
   Michael McNair
   is being so helpful?

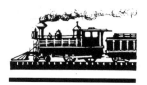

CHAPTER 5

Michael McNair
set up the McGees
with a room in town.
He even
took them there.
He set up jobs
for both of them.
He told them
how to get to work.
He told them
about a woman
who lived
on the next street.
For a little money,
she took care
of children
while the parents
went to work.

Then the man asked
for money.

Johnny gave it
to him.

"Good luck!"
said Michael McNair.
"God be with you,
you two greenhorns!"

After Michael McNair left,
Johnny turned to Mary.
"Did that seem
like a lot of money?"

"Yes, Johnny,
it did,"
said Mary.
"Perhaps McNair
put one over on us.
But what else
could we do?
We needed help.
And he was there
to help us."

"Ah, but I
did not think

an Irishman would do this,"
said Johnny.

"Maybe someday
it won't seem
like a lot of money,"
said Mary.
"We will work.
We will make
good money.
We will have
enough food to eat
every day.
We will be
hungry no more."

"And we won't need
help from somebody
like Michael McNair,"
Johnny added.
"We will
be strong again soon.
We will be able
to take care of ourselves."

Thinking It Over

1. Did anyone ever
   "put one over" on you
   for money?

2. Do you think
   Johnny's and Mary's jobs
   will be easy?

CHAPTER 6

Johnny was away
for months at a time.
There was a railroad
to build.
Johnny McGee
helped to build it.

The work was hard.
Very, very hard.
They gave Johnny
a pick and a shovel.
Johnny dug
into the earth.
He got
the roadbed ready.
He laid rails
into the roadbed.
He drove spikes
into the rails.

He also helped
to blow up rocks
along the way.
This was
the worst work of all.
He had seen
some of his friends
get blown up
along with the rocks.

Johnny began work
when the sun came up.
He did not stop
until the sun went down.

For all of this,
Johnny's pay
was 25 dollars
a month.
But sometimes
the boss
kept the money
for himself.
Some months
Johnny never saw
a cent.

Back in the city
Mary worked
in the mill.
She ran a machine.
The machine
spun wool.
The mill was hot.
Sometimes the wool
hurt Mary's skin.

There was
a bright side
to Mary's job.
She made friends
at the mill.
And she made money.
It wasn't much.
She got paid
even less than Johnny.
But it was all
she could hope for
right now.
The money she made
put food
on her table
every night.

Johnny came home
once every few months.
Mary was so happy
to see him.
Their time together
was very special.

"This is
not an easy life,"
said Johnny.
"We work very hard.
We see each other
very little.
I miss you and Terry
so much."

"I do not mind,"
said Mary.
"Look at this table.
There is food
to eat.
Not just potatoes,
but meat, too!"

"Yes,"
said Johnny.

"That is something
to be glad about.
We have not had
one hungry day
in this new life."

"I think
Father Kerry
would be happy,"
said Mary.
She would never know
whether *he* had had
enough to eat.

Thinking It Over

1. How much
   could you put up with
   as long as you
   had food to eat?

2. What kind of work
   would Johnny get
   if he came to America today?

3. What is your idea
   of a hard job?

CHAPTER 7

Sometimes the railroad workers
would slow down.
"Keep a move on!"
Johnny would say.
Then he would
start a song.
"Sing along with me,"
he would say.
The other men
would join in.
Their picks
would hit the earth
all at the same time.
The picks
kept the beat
of the song.

The railroad company
liked Johnny.
He kept
the other men working.

Besides,
Johnny spoke English.
So when the boss left,
Johnny got his job.
The company
gave him more money.
He didn't have to work
with a pick now.
It was his job
to keep the others busy.

"Keep an eye
on McGee,"
a worker named Murphy
said to the others.
"The boss before him
took our money.
So will McGee."

"I won't take
your money,"
said Johnny McGee.
"I won't be
that kind of boss.
You can be sure of that,
my friend."

But Murphy
kept his eye
on Johnny.
Months went by.
Murphy never saw
Johnny take a cent.

"You are all right, McGee,"
Murphy said one day.
"You are
a good boss.
You make
people work.
But you pay us.
You are a fair man,
Johnny McGee."

Murphy and Johnny
became friends.
They had a drink together
every night.
Murphy became
Johnny's right-hand man.
Johnny knew he could
count on Murphy.

"Tomorrow we'll hit
a big block of rock,"
Murphy told Johnny.
"I think
we should take turns
setting the blowup."

"That's a fair idea,"
said Johnny.

"I'll go first,"
said Murphy.
"I'll set up tomorrow."

So Murphy
set the blowup.
"Ready!"
he called.
He stepped back.
Bang!
Rocks and dust
blew up
toward the sky.
The earth shook.
Then it was over.

The dust
fell back down.

"Where's Murphy?"
Johnny shouted.
He looked around.

Murphy lay
beside the broken rocks.
There was blood
all over him.
He was dead.

Thinking It Over

1. What is your idea
   of a fair boss?

2. Why do you think
   Johnny does not take
   the worker's money?

3. Would you take
   the first turn
   at a dangerous job?

CHAPTER **8**

Johnny went to Boston
a few weeks later.

"I have a surprise!"
said Mary.

"No need to tell me,"
said Johnny.
"I can see!
There is another baby
on the way!"

"I had to leave
the mill,"
said Mary.
"I cannot work now.
But at least
I will be able to
keep Terry
at home with me."

"I want to stay
in Boston,"
said Johnny.
"I want to be here
for our family.
I know I can
find work here."

So Johnny
began to work
for the city.
He got a job
as a policeman.
"I could not help Murphy,"
he said.
"But maybe
I can help other people."

A few months later
the baby was born.
"We will name him
James Murphy McGee,"
said Johnny.

Life in the city
was new to Johnny.

Until now,
he did not know
how bad things were.
Some people from Ireland
could not pay rent.
A whole family
lived in a small house
made of an old box.
There were
many fires.
Many people
lost the poor homes
they had.

   "We must
do what we can
to help these people,"
said Johnny.
So he became
a firefighter, too.
He joined
a group of men
who put out fires
for no pay.
When the bell went off,
Johnny ran.

Sometimes
two fire groups
showed up
at the same fire.
Both groups wanted
to put out the fire.
A fight
would break out
between the groups.
Sometimes
a house burned
to the ground
while the fight went on.

"This is silly,"
said Johnny.
"Each group
should fight fires
in their own
part of town."

"You are
a good leader,"
Donald O'Neal told Johnny.
O'Neal was the leader
of a political party

in Boston.
"You should become
a ward heeler."

And so he did.
As a ward heeler,
Johnny did many things.
He found jobs
for new people.
He got people
out of jail.
He sent flowers
when someone died.
Johnny was doing
what he wanted to do.
He was helping people.
He got paid
to be a policeman.
But he was also
a firefighter
and a ward heeler.
In everything he did,
he was helping people.

Another baby
was on the way.

The McGee family
moved to a bigger place.
When the baby
was born,
Johnny and Mary
named her Megan.
For the next five years
there was
a new baby
each year.

Thinking It Over

1. What do you do
   to help other people?

2. Can you think of a way
   to make your town
   work better?

3. What makes
   a good leader?

CHAPTER **9**

More and more Irish people
came to Boston.
Some Americans
were not happy
about it.

"The Irish
are taking our jobs!"
they said.
"They are lazy!
They drink
on Saturday night!
Their church
is no good!
Down with the Irish!"

Fights broke out.
The police
had to break them up.

The Americans
did not like
Irish policemen.
They called Johnny
mean names.

"The Boston mothers
won't let their children
play with our children,"
Mary told Johnny.
"Just yesterday,
Megan told me
two of her little friends
weren't speaking to her.
What should we do?"

"Let it be,"
said Johnny.
"Be very careful
with the children.
Keep them
with Irish children.
We don't want them
to get hurt.
They should play

in the churchyard.
They will be
safe there."

In the summer
the McGee children
played every day.
One hot day
they were playing
in the churchyard.
They ran
round and round
between stones and flowers.
They played
silly games.
Only Irish children
were there.

All of a sudden
a group of men
stormed into the yard.
They shouted
and waved sticks
in the air.
The children screamed.

"Get away!"
called the men.
"We do not want
to hurt you!"

The men
ran into the church.
The children
stood still.
They heard
the sound of breaking wood.
They heard
the crash of stone
against the floor.
The children
were afraid to move.
What were these men
doing inside the church?

Then they heard
the men leaving
by the other door.

The children
walked inside the church.

It was a mess.
Wood and stone
lay in pieces.
It was
an ugly sight.

"We must go home,"
said Megan McGee.
"We must tell Mother
what we saw."

Thinking It Over

1. Why would people wreck
   someone else's place?

2. How would you explain
   to the children
   what happened?

3. Is there ever
   a good reason
   to hate a group of people?

CHAPTER **10**

"Why did the men
do such a mean thing?"
asked Megan McGee.
"They made a mess
of our church."

"What you saw
was hate,"
explained Mary McGee.
"Hate is
a very bad thing.
These people
hate the Irish
and our church.
Don't ever hate anyone.
Don't ever hurt anyone.
Don't ever become
so angry."

Mary and Johnny
helped to fix the church.

They gave money.
They made new seats.
They cut new stone.
It took a year.
But the church
looked like new.
They never found out
who made the mess.

"Now it is time
to get ready
for the war,"
said Johnny.

There was a war
going on in America.
The North
was fighting
against the South.
The North wanted
to free the slaves.
The South did not.

"I don't want
to free the slaves,"
said Johnny.

"Why not?"
asked Megan.

"I am afraid
they will take
our jobs,"
said her father.

"Do you hate
the slaves?"
asked the little girl.

"No,"
Johnny said.
"But the Irish
have a hard enough time.
We need our jobs."

"But why
must you fight
in the war?"
asked Megan.
"Mother told us
never to hate.
She told us
never to hurt anyone."

"We have no choice.
We must fight
to save the North!"
Johnny explained.
"The North
is our home.
We cannot let
the South win the war."

So Johnny
put together
a fighting group.
He and his Irish friends
marched together.
They learned
to fight.
Each man
carried his own gun.
Before long,
the group was ready.
It was time
to march off to war.

Thinking It Over

1. How do you feel
   about war?
   Is there ever
   a good reason
   to fight?

2. What is the difference
   between what the men did
   to the church
   and fighting in a war?

3. Have you ever
   worked with other people
   to build or make something big?

CHAPTER **11**

Once again
Mary was home
without her husband.
This time,
there were eight children
to take care of.
Mary had to run the house
by herself.
And once again,
the family
needed money.

"I must find
a job,"
she told the children.
"Go get me
a newspaper.
I must find out
who needs
a houseworker."

She read
the list of jobs
in the newspaper.
WOMAN WANTED.
All kinds
of housework.
No Irish.
NEED WOMAN.
To clean house
and care for children.
No Irish.
HOUSEMAID.
Work all around the house.
No Irish.

"What shall I do?"
Mary wondered.
There were lots
of jobs.
But no one
wanted an Irish woman
to work for them.

Mary did not give up.
"I'll just show them
who I am,"

she said.
She picked up
the newspaper.
She slammed
the door
on her way out.

She knocked
on the first door.
A woman
answered the knock.

"I understand
you need
a housemaid,"
said Mary.
"I know
how to clean.
I have
eight children.
My husband
is off at war.
I will do
very good work.
May I
have the job?"

The woman
looked Mary over.
"You seem
clean enough,"
she said.
"My name is
Mrs. Brock.
Come in."

The woman
never asked
if Mary was Irish.
"I need someone
right away,"
she said.
"When can you start?"

Thinking It Over

1. Did you ever
   not like someone
   before you met them?
   Did you
   change your mind
   when you met them?

2. Could what happened to Mary
   happen today?

CHAPTER **12**

Every morning
Mary woke up
before the sun
came up.
Every morning
she walked
to work.
The Brocks lived
four miles across town.

Mary cleaned
the Brock house.
She cooked
for the Brock family.
She took care
of the three Brock children.

She got home
after the sun went down.
Then she cleaned
the McGee house.

She cooked
for the McGee family.
She took care
of the eight McGee children.

Her Johnny
was on her mind
all the time.
She was afraid.
She knew
Johnny was brave.
But even brave men
can die in a war.

Every now and then
a letter came
from Johnny.
Sometimes the letters
were many months old.
Perhaps Johnny
was still all right
two months ago.
But Mary never knew
if another letter
was on its way.

Mary read
each letter
out loud
to the children.

"My dear family,"
wrote Johnny.
"Yesterday ended
the Battle of Bull Run.
We marched
into battle.
We waved
our green Irish flag.
We did not win.
But don't let
anyone tell you
the Irish are
afraid to fight.
We are brave.
We fight hard.
We have lost
many men
in this war.
Tom McCann
lost a leg

for the North.
But I am safe.
Do not worry.
I will be home soon."

"He *will* come home,"
Mary said
to herself.
"My Johnny McGee
will come home.
I must believe it."

Thinking It Over

1. Do you hope
   for the best
   or wait for the worst?

2. What is your idea
   of being brave?

CHAPTER **13**

"Still another man
from Boston
has been killed!"
said Mr. Brock.

"Oh, how sad!"
said Mary.
"Did the man
have a family?"

"I believe so,"
said Mr. Brock.
"They live
over on Cross Street."

"Oh, the poor family,"
said Mary.
She could not say
what was on her mind.
She was glad

the dead man
was not Johnny.

   "The war
cannot last long,"
Mr. Brock added.
"The South
is finished.
They will give up.
It is only
a matter of time."
Mr. Brock
left the room.
Then he stepped out
into the street.

   Mary could think
only of her husband.
She washed
the kitchen floor.
She heard his name
in every push
of the mop.
Johnny.
Johnny.
Johnny.

All of a sudden
Mr. Brock
came back into the house.
He ran into the kitchen.
There was a big smile
on his face.
"Good news, Mary!"
he shouted.
"The war is over!
The word is out!
Our men
are on their way home!"

Mary dropped
the mop.
She held
her hands together.
"Oh, thank God!
Please may my Johnny
be safe!"

Thinking It Over

1. Why do you think
   Mr. Brock
   is not in the war?

2. What is it like
   to wonder
   if someone is OK?

3. Do you think
   Johnny will come home?

CHAPTER **14**

Weeks went by.
There was
no word from Johnny.
Maybe he
was on his way home.
Maybe he
was hurt.
Or maybe he
was dead.

None of the Irish group
had come home yet.
No one else
had heard any news.

Then one day
Mary was walking
home from work.
It was
almost dark.
She heard

the soft beat
of a drum.
The sound
was coming
from way down the street.
The beat
got louder.
And louder.
And louder.

Mary looked
as hard as she could.
The drum beat
was very loud now.
Then she saw
a row of heads
pop up
from over
the top of the hill.

People began
to come out of their houses.
The street
filled with people.
The row of heads

became rows of men.
The men
marched down the street.
One of them
beat the drum.
They looked
tired and dirty.
Some walked
with crutches.

Mary ran
up the street.
She ran
until she could see
every face.
She looked
at every man
that passed by.
She saw
faces she knew.
Where was Johnny?

A man in front
waved his hand.
"Mary!"
he called.

Mary's heart
skipped a beat.
Could this
be Johnny?
This man
had long hair.
He had
a beard, too.
And his clothes
were in rags.

"Mary!"
he called again.

"Johnny!"
called Mary.
"Of course,
it is you!
Of course,
you came home!
Of course,
you are walking
right up front!"

"Yes, and
I can't believe

I am home!"
said Johnny.

   His voice
sounded weak.
He looked thin.
His arm
was hurt.
But he was
in one piece.
And he was home.
Johnny came marching home.

   Boston threw
a big party.
The North
had won the war.
The Irish group
had helped.

   "What will you
do now?"
Mary asked Johnny.

   "I want to run
for city office,"

said Johnny.
"I want
to help run
this city."

And so he did.
Johnny McGee
became a big name
in Boston.
Mary took care
of the family.
Every night
she cooked
a hot dinner.

Johnny and Mary
did not live
to be old.
Their bodies were
worn out
from hard work.
But they died happy,
not hungry.
And the country
was better off
because of them.

Thinking It Over

1. What did these Irish people give to the country?

2. Why do people run for office?

3. What will you leave behind when you are gone?